CUFFED TO A SAVAGE

LOVING A SAVAGE BOOK 1

MIA BLACK

CHAPTER 1

"Make sure you wear that badge with pride. It means something, Mathis," repeated Officer Brantwell. The first three times he said it, I actually responded. Once I realized that each of his speeches was going to end with it, I just nodded and mumbled something. "It means something…"

I looked down at the extra sharp creases on the pants of my navy blue uniform and then over to the radar gun that was perched in the window. It went off again, showing yet *another* person going at the speed limit. Glancing around the hot car, I couldn't imagine the detectives on TV doing shit like this. Imagine them trying to put Olivia Benson on speed patrol.

I was excited to be starting my new job that morning so I'd sent my mother a picture of the uniform before I put it on and of course she asked for one after, too.. She'd sent me back a whole screen full of emojis and words telling me how proud of me she was. She also told me that I should take it easy. That wasn't hard at all. Day one on the job wasn't going how I expected it to, not at all.

When I first got my uniform, I cried like a damn baby. If you knew me, you knew that I didn't really think I'd make it all the way through the Academy. In fact, my mother and other people had tried their hardest to talk me out of it, but I kept on going. I'd always been a little bit stubborn and I hated it when people told me I couldn't do something. I'd used their words to keep pushing me through and it finally paid off.

I would have loved to tell you that I had some noble reason for wanting to join the NYPD, but I didn't. I was in debt and needed the money. It's guaranteed hours, benefits, all that. I figured that If I liked it then I could do it for a couple of years and move on. I was only

23 so it wasn't like I didn't have time ahead of me, God willing.

My expectations for the job in general were high and I was expecting to hit the ground running. I watched a lot of TV. I loved cop shows! Law and Order: SVU and The Wire were two of my favorite shows. Hell, I even watch the reruns of New York Undercover when I could catch them. I knew that it was the detectives that got the most action but I knew that beat cops were usually the first ones on the scene and saw a lot too.

"You're tough," Brantwell said. "I can see that in you. Plus you did what a lot of people can't do which is make it out of the Academy. Some guys might try and use the fact that you're a woman to their advantage and you can't let them. You're pretty too. Learn to use that."

I tried not to roll my eyes at him. I'd had a couple of people tell me that I was "too pretty" to be a police officer which didn't make any sense to me because I'd seen plenty of cops who were baddies. I'd also had people tell me that I was too nice to be a cop, citing my normally bubbly personality.

I was 5'6" with smooth cinnamon colored

skin. My almond shaped eyes were warm and brown, the color of chestnuts. My long, reddish brown hair was naturally curly and usually hung at my shoulders but I tied it up in a ponytail. I was one of those slim thick shaped girls. I had a nice ass and breasts and they were in proportion with my size and not overly huge the way that had become the trend.

I was expecting to be walking the New York streets or at least riding around in them, waiting for a call about a rape or murder, at least a robbery, *something*. Instead, my ass was in a car, parked on the side of the highway in a speed trap. I didn't know how long it would be before I'd be able to get out and see some real action and when I asked Officer Brantwell, he made it clear that it can sometimes take a while and that it's a "process that can't be rushed," whatever that means.

Officer Jim Brantwell was my Field Training Officer, or FTO for short. He was 45 years old and looked like a stereotypical police officer: white male, 6'1 with a stocky build. Jim had thick, muscular arms and his stomach had a little pudge but it looked like it had been flat at one time. I'd heard stories about how a lot of

FTOs could be assholes to try and scare us newbies but Jim had been cool so far. Boring as hell, but cool.

Yet another car drove by, a blue BMW. The light hit it and I was glad that I had on sunglasses. I looked down at the radar with my hopes up but got them let back down when I saw that it was going at the speed limit.

"Did you hear me?" Officer Brantwell asked.

I turned my head to him. I'd been staring at the blue beamer as it passed. It looked like it was going somewhere exciting and for a minute I just wanted to be inside of it, riding to wherever they were going.

"Yeah," I said with a nod. I cleared my throat. It was warm inside the car. "I heard you."

He looked at me for a second then then kept right on talking and staring out the window. I hadn't heard any of what his ass had been talking about but I just nodded every few seconds like I was paying attention.

"Now, I know that the NYPD can get a bad rap at times. People don't like to talk about it. My father and my uncles didn't like to talk about it but shit happens sometimes and we get the blame. Sometimes it's our fault. Sometimes it isn't. The thing is this: the public needs to trust us and we need to earn their trust," Officer Brantwell was saying. I was only halfway paying attention to him when he was interrupted by the loud beeping of the radar gun.

My head snapped to the left. I saw a car zooming by and the radar said that it was going 20 miles over the speed limit. My heartbeat sped up and I sat up a little in my chair. Brantwell's hands were already moving, putting the car into drive.

"OK, Officer Mathis," he said. He had a gleam of excitement in his eyes. "Let's go catch some bad guys." It was a corny line but I could tell that he'd gotten a kick out of using it.

Brantwell put the car into drive and we pulled out of the spot quickly. We sped down the road, trying to catch up with the black car and its driver. It was exciting as hell to be the cop in the car, watching the cars move out of the way as the sirens came on and blared.

Brantwell said that we were about to go catch "bad guys" and I knew that was the point of the job but we were just chasing someone who'd gone above the speed limit, not a criminal mastermind. Shit, before I became a cop, I loved to speed. The quicker I could get somewhere, the better. I put that stuff in the back of my mind though as I enjoyed the thrill of the chase. We caught up the car and it began to slow down and pull over the side of the road as we did the same.

Brantwell turned to me as we both took off our seat belts. "Just hang back and play the passenger's side, OK? Watch how I handle this guy, alright?" He had a serious look on his face.

"OK," I said with a nod. As excited as I was for action, I wasn't gonna be stupid about it. Brantwell had more years on the job than I'd been alive so I planned on listening to him with this.

We both got out of the car. I peered through the back of the car but I couldn't really see the people on either side. Brantwell looked a little tense but was mostly relaxed. I followed his movements as we both made our way up the sides of the car. I hung back a little back, approaching the passenger side door a little slower than he was doing to the driver's side.

I was annoyed once I got into viewing

distance of the driver and spotted that sitting in both the driver's and passenger's seats were nothing but two 30 something women who both looked pissed off. The black car that I'd seen go by in a blur was actually a navy blue van. We'd pulled over two soccer moms. I wanted to roll my eyes at it all as I watched Brantwell start speaking to the driver.

"Ma'am, you were doing about 20 miles over the speed limit," Brantwell said. He peered into the car.

"I wasn't speeding!" she said. "Was I speeding?" She turned to her friend. Her friend shook her head and I was almost afraid it was gonna come off her head.

"Ma'am, our radar showed you going over the speed limit. You can't deny that. Me and my partner both saw it," he said. He looked to me for confirmation and I nodded my head nervously while trying not to make eye contact with the driver or passenger.

"We're kind of in a rush," said the driver. She sucked her teeth. I could tell that she was over it but she just pulled out her license and registration and handed them to Brantwell. "Here you go."

"Thanks," Brantwell said.

He turned and headed back to our car. I followed behind him. Brantwell ran the driver's license and everything else but I could tell by the looks on their faces that we weren't going to find anything. They were probably in a rush to pick up their kids from somewhere and Brantwell's ass was excited as hell to be writing them the ticket. He was smiling and everything.

"Now look," Brantwell began, "sometimes you get these types. They like to argue and stuff but the thing is this: the law is the law. We both saw the radar. And they like to try and fight it sometimes but they're caught!" You would think that he'd have won the lottery. He seemed to be getting real pleasure from all of this.

I just nodded my head. I'd been excited at first about the stop but all that went out the window as soon as I realized that it was just two soccer moms trying to mind their business and get home.

"It's clean," Brantwell said. He sounded kind of disappointed that him running the license and plate had come back without any red flags. "Well, they still get a ticket anyway for the speeding." He wrote out the ticket and

MIA BLACK

pulled it off of the little clip board he held in his hands. I had one too. We used them to write tickets but I hadn't anything but flip through the pages of mine.

We walked back over to the car. I was on alert but I was still a lot more relaxed than I was the first time. Brantwell handed them the ticket. I was standing behind him on the driver's side and I heard the driver mumble a couple of slick things under her breath. I was sure that if I heard them from where I was standing, Brantwell *definitely* heard them, but he didn't say anything.

As we walked back to the car, I couldn't help but think about the fact that I felt like a fucking trainee at McDonald's or Applebee's or something like that. I'd had my fair share of odd jobs growing up so I knew what it was like to work at either of those places. You got treated like a kid. You couldn't touch anything and you had to follow behind some other person who was more experienced but usually hated someone shadowing them like a lost child.

I hated situations like that and that was exactly what this felt like. As the trainee, you were usually either doing one of two things. You could just be playing the back, standing in the cut looking goofy. That was what I'd been doing when we went to the car the second time. If you weren't doing that, then you were allowed to at least *feel* like you were in control because you actually got to do something. I say feel because you were only doing things under the watchful eye of your trainer who was waiting to step in and tell you that you'd fucked up somehow.

I wondered if the driver of the car had known that it was my first day. Whenever you went places, you could usually spot the trainee. They were focused just a little bit harder on everything but more than anything, there was always a fear of messing up. I knew that I was feeling that too, even if I didn't wanna admit it.

The rest of the day was almost interesting. We caught three more speedsters: another soccer mom, a bunch of college students, and a guy in a business suit. The guy in the suit had been the most interesting because he'd argued with Brantwell saying that he wasn't going that fast. In the end he just accepted the ticket and drove off after throwing it out the window. I wanted to laugh but I kept it to myself.

I thought that we'd just head back to patrol

to drop off the car and go home but Brantwell brought me to a coffee shop. I got excited about it because it was finally starting to feel like something out of the shows I'd watched. The bar was full of fellow officers. There were regular patrons too but it was clear that this place was a place where the police hung out.

Brantwell greeted a lot of people, including the workers, by name. Once the two of us were seated the waitress came over. She greeted Brantwell and introduced herself to me as Theresa. She looked like she was in her mid 30's. She had olive colored skin with jet black hair. She could have been Italian or Spanish.

"What's your name, sweetheart?" Theresa asked. I lied her. I could tell that she was good at her job because she had a naturally friendly nature about herself.

"Officer Mathis," I replied.

Theresa shook her head. "Your first name. This place is like home."

I smiled. "I'm Taela but everyone just calls me Tae," I said.

"I like that," Theresa said with a smile. She asked me how I liked my coffee and I told her light and sweet. She and Brantwell laughed.

"What?" I asked once Theresa walked away.

"It's just that all the rookies come in and have all these different orders and if they make it in a couple of years, we all drink pretty much the same thing," Brantwell said.

"And what's that?" I was curious to know.

"For me it's black coffee, two sugars. Some people have no sugars, more sugars. At the end of some days, I might add a little whiskey depending on what kinda shit I've seen that day. Some people add whiskey all the time but that's just between us," he said. He smiled at me and I smiled back. Brantwell was boring but at least he was filling up the silence that would have otherwise fallen.

Theresa came back over and brought out coffees. She asked us what we wanted to order and I told Brantwell that he could order first. I was excited to see him order. I just needed to see if he was going to live up to my expectations.

"The pie looks good. I was eyeing it when I came in," Brantwell said with a chuckle.

I rolled my eyes, thankful that neither of them had seen it. He couldn't even order a damn donut? What kind of mess was this? I'd been expecting him to be chowing down on something with sprinkles on it with his coffee, not pie.

Theresa turned to me, asking about my order.

"I'll have one of those strawberry frosted donuts with the sprinkles," I said.

"Sounds good," Theresa smiled as she walked away.

When she came back with the food, I half listened to Brantwell talk about something. I had to chuckle to myself that I had to be the one to get the donut; the irony of it all. Being a police officer wasn't shaping up to be what I'd thought it would.

CHAPTER 2

I'D GONE HOME at the end of what turned out to be a long day and even though what I really wanted was just to relax with a bottle of wine and only hear the sound of fine ass Omari Hardwick on *Power*, I had to recap day with everyone. My phone didn't stop blowing up. I finally put it on Do Not Disturb and made sure my alarm was set. I had an early start the next day. There would be plenty of time for me to catch up with them and let them know how work had gone.

At 5:20 in the morning I was walking into the station in my street clothes. I needed to be dressed and ready for roll call by 6 so I got there a little early. I wanted to try and introduce myself to people but the last thing I was about to be was friendly that early in the morning. I was making my way to the female locker room to drop my bag off and go change when a commotion caught my attention.

Somebody was being booked and was supposed to just be sitting on the bench waiting for their turn to be processed. I was trying to just go about my business but whoever it was, they were putting on a show. I was nosey as hell and decided to see what was going on. I walked over to the other side of the room and found the source of the deep voice. He had two officers on him. They'd just taken their hands off of him. His hands were cuffed behind his back.

There were a couple of columns in the room and I was standing behind one of them. I was halfway hidden but I had a view of what happening.

"Yo! I'm good! I'm not sitting on the bench though," he said. His back was facing me but his 6'4" frame and deep voice gave off the impression of power. It was clear that this was a man who was used to giving orders and not taking them.

He turned around and it was then that I

realized that I was only standing 10 feet from one of the most beautifully rugged creatures that I'd ever seen before. He was beautiful because his smooth skin was the color of milk chocolate and looked like it was glowing in the fluorescent lights of the room. He looked like he'd never had any acne or anything like that, just smoothing skin his entire life. He had dark brown hair that was cut in a low Caesar fade. He had just the right amount of facial hair: a five o'clock shadow beard that was cut low to the face and framed his full lips.

The ruggedness came from the colorful tattoos that were all along his body, framing his muscular arms. Some of them looked so realistic that they might have jumped off his arms at me. He had on a short sleeved shirt and the top buttons were open. Green and red flowers, black crosses, all kinds of colors were on the tattoos that traced him. Thankfully he didn't have any on his face and two small ones on his neck.

I was sure that I'd never met him before. I would have remembered meeting him. He had a presence about him and I knew that If I'd seen him it would have left an impression on me. It was strange that I felt something familiar about him. It was like I knew him from some other life or something like that. I know that it sounded crazy but it was true.

I walked a little bit closer to him. The cops had put their hands on him and he was struggling against them.

"This is some bullshit!" he said. "I'm letting you all know this: I'll have the badges of every person involved in this." His voice was rough and demanding and he was speaking like he meant every word of what he'd just said.

He was struggling against the police but somehow he and I managed to lock eyes. There was a jolt of electricity that hit my body so intensely that I took another step forward. His intense brown eyes were staring into mine and I felt my whole body get warm. It wasn't just me. Whatever was happening, he was feeling it too. It was like time had stopped and was only just starting to move again, crawling by the nanosecond.

And then the moment seemed to end because something in his eyes flickered and time caught all the way up to us. It was like he'd realized that he'd been staring for too long and needed to get back into character. His eyes ducked to the ground as he started fussing and struggling the police again.

I also realized that I'd just been having a staring contest with a guy who was getting booked and it was only my second day on the job. I needed to keep my head in the game. I turned and scurried away, heading towards the locker room to change into my uniformed.

In the locker room I was taking my time while I got dressed, making sure that everything looked right as I put it on. Whoever that dude had been he'd definitely made an impression on me. I tried to push him out of my mind though and focus on the day ahead of me.

I'd been thinking about it on my way to work that morning and I couldn't help but think that maybe I'd been the one who'd fucked up my first day. I'd come into the job with all of these expectations and things and got upset when they didn't work out the way I expected them to. I felt much more prepared for day two because I knew what I should be expecting. I was trying to improve my attitude.

I double checked myself one last time in the mirror before I headed to the briefing room to hear about what was going on for the day. It was our time to get information on what crimes had been committed, big arrests, statistics, stuff like that.

I hated to admit it but I really wanted to see that dude again. It was pretty much a straight shot from the locker room to the briefing room but I purposely went out of my way to see if I could see him again.

I looked over at the benches and he was seated there. His hands were cuffed behind his back and his head was resting against the wall with his eyes closed. I walked slowly up to him since I'd have to pass right in front of him to get to the briefing room down the hall.

Right before I got over in front of him his eyes opened. He looked at me and his eyes got wide as hell. I was confused but I remembered that when he'd seen me a little while ago I'd been wearing my street clothes so he might have thought I was a civilian. I was now dressed in the traditional navy blue of the NYPD.

He recovered from his shock quickly though. His eyes narrowed in a sexy way and he quickly looked up and down my body, tracing my curves. I was staring him in his eyes and he knew it because once again he was staring back at me. He winked at me in a confident way. My eyes darted away from him and hit the floor as I kept on walking. I couldn't get the image out of my mind and my entire body felt hot as I walked down the hall. I could feel his eyes on me.

Ugh! I snapped myself back to reality as I walked into the briefing room and took a seat close to the aisle. I couldn't believe that I was getting so damn dreamy eyed over someone who could potentially be a criminal. On the other hand, he could also just be a guy with a DUI or something.

The bosses came in and the briefings started. I paid attention, even though a lot of it was just numbers that changed by the day about how many arrests, murders, tickets, etc. It was only my second briefing but I wasn't dumb. I felt the mood in the air change and a couple of people in suits walked in. They made everything more tense in the room. Someone in the back flipped the light and it went out.

Up on the screen, a face was projected. It was mugshot and I was shocked to see that it was the guy who I'd been staring at outside. Even in the mugshot his eyes were mesmerizing but instead of the intrigue that filled them when he looked at me, they were full of anger. The nameplate he was holding said his name was Eric Mayfield AKA "Young."

"Eric Mayfield, known on the streets as Young, is a face that a lot of you might recognize. His name comes up a lot and we haven't been able to make anything stick. He's here tonight because of a routine stop that got a little rowdy. We searched the car and found nothing, same as always. He'll be out by morning but he's ours tonight," explained one of the suits that had just walked into the room. He was old, in his 50's and had a full head of white hair and a belly that looked like it wasn't touching the floor because it was being held back by his shirt.

"Be on the lookout. He is a dangerous man. He's the leader of the notorious AB Boys gang who run much of Harlem and he has his hand in a lot of illegal things. We want you all to keep your ears to the streets because he has people all over and we're close. We just need a slip up," he said. He paused and looked around the room. He went on. He clicked through a slideshow of different crime scenes all either associated directly with Eric or his gang. The crime scenes varied: drugs, money, murder, etc. It was a lot.

As Brantwell and I headed out that day to give out more tickets, I focused on doing my job as much as I could. I got the chance to give out a couple of tickets myself.

In the back of my mind I couldn't help but to think about Young. We'd only had two very brief encounters but dude had left a major impression on me. I couldn't say that I was feeling him because I'd only just gotten to know him but I was definitely intrigued. I had to remind myself a bunch of times that he was a dangerous guy and that my job and his line of work conflicted. As the day went on, I pushed thoughts of him out of my mind and focused on making the most out of day two on the job.

CHAPTER 3

My first week on the job had been long, longer than I thought it would be. When Saturday came around, I knew that I was ready to relax but also knew that I wasn't gonna get the chance to. It would have been nice to have stayed in my bed and just slept in but I had to get up and get dressed. Nana, as the family called her, was my grandmother on my mother's side and it was her 87th birthday party that day. My mother and aunt were throwing it so they decided to have it early in the day so that Nana would still be up. She could move around great for her age but she also wasn't a night owl either so the earlier the better.

I threw on a pair of jeans and a t-shirt, placing my actual outfit in a bag. I'd bought my grandmother a gift as well: a beautiful white church hat and a pearl necklace to go with it I knew that she'd love them both. She never missed church and was very old school with her fashions too, wearing a different hat every Sunday. I'd gone with her a couple of times and she was well liked and respected around her church.

I could have driven but I decided to take the bus instead. New Rochelle wasn't too far from my Harlem apartment and it wasn't going to take me that long to get there. I got on the bus a little before noon and found a seat in the middle. I sat down next to the window and placed the gift and my bag next to me. I started glancing out the window. I was trying hard to make sure that no one came and sat next to me.

I was sitting watching the line of people coming onto the bus get shorter. We were waiting to pull off when someone's deep voice spoke to me and snapped me from me my thoughts.

"Is this seat taken?" someone asked. I rolled

my eyes. Clearly I'd put my stuff there for a reason. I turned around and was about to give whoever it was the most attitude because I *knew* the bus wasn't full but once I looked up, all those thoughts left me.

Standing in front of me with skin the deep brown color of toffee and a head of curly brown hair was a man—a handsome one too. He was smiling at me with a set of perfectly white teeth and full lips. His hazel eyes were staring down at me.

"No!" I said quickly. I snatched up my stuff and practically threw it on the floor in front of me. My grandmother's hat was in a box and wasn't gonna fit on the floor, and I wasn't about to hold it for the entire ride.

"Need help?" The guy asked.

"Yes," I smiled up at him. "Would you mind placing this box up top please?" I handed it to him and he placed it in the compartment above our seats. He sat down next to me.

"Thanks," I said. After a couple of minutes of silence the bus pulled off.

"I'm Reggie," said the guy next to me. He turned to me a little bit and extended his hand to me. I put mine out and he grabbed it tightly in mine. His hands were huge. "Nice to meet you."

"Tae," I said with a smile. "Nice to meet you too."

"So where are you headed?" He asked me. "New Rochelle or someplace before it?"

"New Rochelle," I said. "And you?"

"Same," he smiled at me. "What are you heading up there for if you don't mind me asking?"

Reggie didn't seem like a creep. He had all his teeth, didn't smell, and seemed like he was actually sane. He was more than just a nice face so I decided to indulge him in conversation, plus he was fine as hell so I was about to turn down a chance to stare at his perfect skin and strong jawline.

"I have a family thing," I said. I didn't need to go into details or anything because I didn't know him.

"Me too," he said. He didn't seem like a creep and had only checked me out once or twice, which was good.

Reggie and I spoke for the rest of the time we were on the bus. We kept it light, getting to know one another as best we could in the time it

MIA BLACK

took for us to drive. He was actually cool. He made me laugh a couple of times with some jokes. We got off the bus right behind one another and we were about to head our separate ways when he suggested that we exchange numbers. I was with it since we'd been talking for so long. I put his number into my phone and then headed out to the parking lot to meet my mother, Marion.

I had my hands full as I walked over. Between my purse, the bag with my clothes, and the box that held my grandmother's gift, I couldn't handle anything else in my hands so I hoped that my mother had parked somewhere visible. I was wandering around the lot looking for her.

"Tae!" I heard a scream that made me snap around. "Over here, baby!" My mother was about three rows of cars behind me. Her hands were in the air and the scream that she'd let out was embarrassing as hell. I quickly walked over to her, trying my hardest to keep my head down. I hoped that Reggie hadn't seen, or heard her. Even for a mom who hadn't seen their kid in a little bit, she was a bit over the top.

My mother was my best friend, hands

28

down. It was just her and I growing up since my father had split soon after she gave birth to me. My mother never let it get her down. She worked hard to put a roof over my head and clothes on my back. We had a great relationship, so great that people sometimes thought we were friends and not mother and daughter. It also didn't hurt that although my mother was 43 years old, she didn't look like it. Her smooth, cinnamon skin barely had any wrinkles. She usually wore her hair natural in either flat twists or some other protective style. She had one or two gray streaks but she refused to dye them, claiming that they gave her some personality.

I had to put the box and stuff down on the hood of the car because as soon as I got within two yards of her, my mother launched herself at me to hug me. She grabbed me tightly and I wrapped my arms around her too, taking in her scent. After almost a full minute of hugging we parted and I stepped back to admire her. She was wearing a cranberry colored wrap dress and black shoes. My girl looked good.

"You look good, Ma," I said to her.

"Like mother, like daughter," she said with a

smile as she looked me up and down. "Let's get you settled so we can be on our way."

She picked up the box that the hat was in. "A new hat? You always know what to get. I can't wait for her to open it," she said.

"Me too. I think she's gonna love it," I said.

The party was happening at Nana's house so my mother was driving the two of us there. As we made our way, she caught me up on all the happenings of my family. She told me about who'd be there, who wouldn't and why, and if I got cornered by which family members what I should do. You know how black family gatherings could be.

"Now look, I have to warn you about this," my mother said in a serious tone.

"What?" I asked.

"Most of the family is happy for you You're doing things right...getting a good job and stuff like that. But you know how your cousins are and you know some of them been to jail before..." My mother's voice trailed off.

"Ma, you can just say it," I said.

"I'm not saying nothing," my mother said. "All I'm saying is just go in here and be aware. I don't wanna have to get outta character with nobody."

I shook my head. "It won't get that serious," I said. "We all just here for Nana."

"Be that as it may," my mother said, "I just want you to handle everyone with care. You know that sometimes people can start talking before they even think about what they're saying."

"I know," I said. When I got accepted to the Police Academy, I thought a lot about what it would mean to be a police officer, especially in the current political state of affairs. Like I said, I hadn't had the best reasons for wanting to join the force but I did at least respect the badge and what it meant. A couple of my cousins had been to jail, some for a long time, and I knew that they couldn't be happy about my decision.

We pulled into the driveway outside Nana's house. I grabbed my things and started to get out of the car when the front door flung open. My Aunt Trina stepped out and started making her way to the car.

Aunt Trina was older than my mother by three years. The two of them were close, although they did have some sibling rivalry but it was nothing crazy. Aunt Trina was married to her second husband, Uncle Mike. They'd been married for such a long time. She looked just like my mother but was a little bit lighter than her. She wore her hair tied back in a ponytail.

"There she is, my favorite niece!" Aunt Trina exclaimed. Aunt Trina could be a little shady at times. I never minded her calling me her favorite but I bet that some of my female cousins did.

I wrapped my arms around her and hugged her tightly and pulled her close to me. My aunt and I were mad cool so it was nothing but love whenever I saw her. "How are you, baby?" she asked me.

"I'm good," I said. "What's going on with you?"

"Nothing much," she said. "Keeping those people at my job in line and what not. You know how I am."

Aunty Trina worked as a supervisor at the phone company, and not one of the small ones either. She had her own office and everything, having worked her way up for twenty years right out of college.

"I feel that," I said.

"I bet you do," she said as she took some of the stuff from my hands and started to hands it off to be taken inside. I'd barely even noticed them but a bunch of my little cousins had come out. They were all in various ages from around 6 to 12 and there were a lot of them, some I recognized and a lot I didn't. You know that in black families the number of cousins you had always went up and down.

"Tell us all about your first week," Aunty Trina said.

"Yeah, Tae, tell us," said one of my cousins.

"Come on Tae Tae," said another.

"Well y'all, it wasn't that interesting," I said honestly. I knew that they probably had high hopes about my stories and stuff but I didn't have any. Outside of a couple of tickets and hearing Brantwell's boring ass stories, I didn't see much action.

"What happened? Did you carry a gun, like even though you're new?" asked Davon, my 11 year old cousin. He was heavy into football and video games. I thought he had a little temper on him but I just kept it to myself.

"Yes, I have one. It's at home right now," I

said. They had a lot of reactions from sad to disappointed.

"Aww man, you should have brought it," Davon said. He slapped his hands on his thighs as we walked into the house.

"Nope, too many kids like you around," I said. I was telling the truth too. I loved my family dearly but I also knew that every now and then something could come up missing from a purse or pocket and no one would have any explanations.

"Tae Tae, did you catch any bad guys?" Charmaine asked. She was eight years old and had always called me Tae Tae. I never tried to stop her either.

"No real bad guys," I said as I walked through the house with my entourage of kids. They followed me as I put my bag down and then walked with me to put the gift with the others. "I did see a lot of speeding cars but that was about it."

Wouldn't you know that they hung onto my every word? I kept on telling them about how my week went and they listened to every single thing that I said like I was telling the greatest story in the world.

I finished telling them about my day and then told the kids that I had stuff to do but I'd come and hang with them later. The party wasn't starting for a little while and there was still a decent amount of stuff to be done. I headed into the kitchen to help my mom, aunts, and older cousins cook and clean up. Nana wasn't there. It wasn't a surprise party but my old lady wasn't about to miss the chance to make an entrance.

I finished helping out in the kitchen and started putting out the party favors. I asked the kids to help me but had to send some of them back when they started playing around. I went ahead and set up the burners for the food. Once I finished that then I put some of the food out and headed upstairs to change. I'd decided to keep it simple, putting on a burnt orange jumper and ash gray heels.

A little after I got dressed I went downstairs and helped with greeting people. I got the kids to help me with collecting gifts and things cause I was willing to play hostess but I wasn't grabbing onto greasy ass pans and stuff. It was nice to see my family and I picked up the vibe that my mother had been warning me about from a couple of people.

Most of everyone had gotten to the party and people were starting to mix and mingle with one another. We'd had hung a banner that read Happy Birthday Betty. Her name was also on her cake. Nana walked in after a while, making an entrance just as I knew she would. My girl was decked out in a red dress with a matching scarf. She must've just come from getting her hair done because it looked nice. Her full head of white hair was curled and she had on earrings and a necklace.

The party really hit full swing when Nana got there. We had a good time. The party was inside the house and in the backyard so it was nice to be in and out of the house. We had a DJ too and he was playing all the best music, new stuff and old school stuff too. Nana got up and danced a couple of times, shaking herself from side to side like she did. She might have been old but she was still very much full of life.

"You must've been hiding from me or something. You ain't even come over and say hi. That must be something new you picked up as a cop," Nana's slow voice came from behind me. I had

just walked down the hallway from the bathroom and was heading to rejoin the party.

"I'm sorry, Nana," I said. "You just look like
you've been having a good time." I walked over
to her and hugged her and smiled. She hugged
me with her cane in her hand and then stepped
back to take me in.

"You look good, baby," Nana said. "That
new job must be doing you some good. I'm
proud of you."

"Thank you, Nana," I said. "It means a lot
to me." I was telling the truth about it too. My
grandmother was the rock of my family and she
made sure that she always let people know how
she felt. It's one of the benefits of being so old.

"I miss you. Why's it been so long since I
seen you? You done switched up on me?" she
asked.

I shook my head. "Nothing like that. It's just
the new job. I'll come and see you again next
weekend or the one after that."

"I hope so," she said. "You make sure you
get some food, baby. I'll see you around Tae."

"See you Nana," I smiled at her. She headed
down the hallway towards the bathroom

The party kept on going and I was making

the most of it, enjoying my time with my family. It'd been awhile since all of us had been around one another like this so it was nice to just vibe.

I wandered into the dining room after a while to get away from everyone. I loved my family but I just needed a couple of minutes of peace and quiet away from them.

One of my cousins, Darius, was sitting at one of the chairs at the table. I greeted him when I walked in and he half mumbled something.

Darius and I were usually cool. At family gatherings he was usually one of the ones who liked to Spades and I did too. He and I never had any beef so I couldn't understand his attitude. My mother did mention that he'd been arguing with his baby mother more so that might have been it.

I sat down at the table and pulled my phone out, aimlessly scrolling through it. I was just trying to gather myself and chill out but I could feel Darius staring at me. I looked up at him and waited for him to blink or look away but he kept right on staring.

Darius was light skinned with a head of jet black hair that he usually kept curled up. He had a couple of tattoos on his arms but nothing too crazy. Darius had been to jail a couple of times for a few misdemeanors.

"Can I help you?" I asked him. He had a toothpick hanging out of his mouth and he was eyeing me with disgust. I took a sip from the red cup I was drinking from.

"Nah, you can't do nothing for me," he said. "I hear you're one of *them* now." He'd said it like I'd somehow become a different person, someone disgusting or something like that.

"And what is *that* supposed to mean?" I asked. I folded my arms over my chest and eyed him.

"Nothing," he spat. "Just don't let them convince you that Black lives don't matter."

"Sure thing!" I said, my voice dripping with sarcasm.

Darius and I grew up together and he'd seen me get into it with more than a couple of people. I couldn't figure out why he was coming at me the way that he was. My mother's words were in my head and I thought about them before I decided to really go off on him.

I got up and picked up my drink before heading to another part of the house. Darius was bugging out. I didn't become a cop and all of a sudden forget who I was or where I came from. I was born and raised in Harlem and nothing was gonna make me forget that. All I needed was for my family to stay level headed. I wasn't looking for any kind of approval for them; I just didn't want them in my way or on my nerves.

CHAPTER 4

It was Thursday and I was almost done with my second week on the job. It was cool and I felt like I was getting the hang of it, even if it was still mostly just pulling over speedsters. Brantwell had taken me out into the field and let me drive around a little bit to catch some people. I'd had a little mini chase but that had been it. Things still hadn't picked up too much.

A bitch was tired! I thought that because I was still technically in training that it would be a while before I saw any overtime or anything. Nope, I was wrong. They got my ass and that second week saw me sitting behind a desk getting experience doing paperwork and dealing with the public. A lot of people came in trying to report actual crimes but a lot of people just wanted to come in and talk about bullshit, like the old lady who complained that her neighbor was walking her dog and letting it shit in her bushes. I listened to her and let her fill out a report but I knew it wasn't going anywhere further than into a file cabinet.

It was a little after 6 in the evening and I'd just walked out of work. I'd just finished a twelve hour shift and my feet hurt. I needed to get a new man, and his name was Dr. Scholl's.

I pulled out my phone and ordered an Uber. I didn't drive that day and had planned on taking the train but I was just too tired and my feet hurt on top of that. After three minutes the car arrived and I got inside. I didn't do a pool because I didn't need a stranger or two all up in my car with me. I stretched out in the back, throwing my bag on the seat next to me.

"Taela?" the driver asked. He had brown skin and jet black hair. He was a handsome Middle Eastern looking guy in his 30's.

"Yes," I said as he pulled off.

He must have gotten the sense that I didn't want to talk or anything because he looked at me a couple of times in the mirror and ended up just turning on some music. I was cool with that too, because it was gonna be a long ride with all of the rush hour traffic.

I don't know why but my mind started to drift and thought about the two guys that I'd met the week before. Well, one of them had only been an unofficial meeting, but still.

Young, the gang leader from the precinct had definitely made a mark on me. His mesmerizing eyes and the rugged class that he had about himself had drawn me in. That wink that he'd given me let me know that if we saw one another outside of him being in handcuffs that he might be interested in something.

The dude that I probably should have been focusing on more was that guy from the bus, Reggie. He was cute and made me laugh. He seemed like the complete opposite of Young but that was fine with me.

Both of them were handsome and had a certain allure about them. Young oozed power and influence. Something about him seemed dangerous but in a way that I kind of liked. Reggie had been kind and courteous. He'd been a gentleman in the brief time that I'd known him and he made me laugh. Anyone that could do that definitely deserved at least a phone call.

I got home and got settled. I changed into some boy shorts and a tank top and wrapped my hair. I pulled out my phone and debated whether or not I should but I just decided to give Reggie a call.

"Hello?" He answered after a couple of rings.

"Hello? Reggie? It's Tae from the bus the other day," I said. I'd gotten nervous just that quick. I wasn't usually the one to hit the guy up so it was a little weird for me.

"Hey, what's up?" He asked. "Sorry about that. I didn't recognize the number."

"No problem," I said. "How are you?"

Reggie and I ended up talking for almost half an hour. I'd really only planned on talking to him for a couple of minutes while we did that awkward conversation that usually led up to one person asking the other to go on a date.

Reggie wasn't that though. Talking with him was easy because he knew how to listen and how to keep a conversation going. Not to mention that he was hilarious. He kept me cracking up the entire time we were on the phone. Before we got off, we agreed to meet up the following day after work for some drinks and light food somewhere. I told him that he could pick the place and he told me he'd text me in the morning to let me know.

Friday came around a lot quicker than I'd expected it too. I went to bed and it felt like I slept for all of five minutes before my alarm went off. It didn't help that the entire work day seemed to drag. I'd finally gotten out of the speed trap but we'd mostly just been riding around. When calls came in through the radio, we let someone else handle the more serious stuff. Friday had absolutely nothing on though.

I also felt like some high school girl or something like that because I was buzzing while thinking about Reggie. I knew that my date with him was gonna be a good one, plus anything was more interesting than Brantwell talk about a whole bunch of nothing.

Just as he'd promised, Reggie text me in the morning letting me know the address of where we'd meet up later. I'd never been to the particular bar that he mentioned we were going to but I was familiar with the area. I kept on resisting the urge to text him. I didn't wanna seem too thirsty or anything like that. I was working hard to make sure that I didn't get my hopes up, even though it was hard. I was really just trying to pace myself and just take it as it came. I was excited for it though.

When my shift ended I raced back to the locker room so I could change. I'd been out sweating all day so I took a quick bird bath and then got out and headed to my locker. I'd brought an outfit to change into, something better than the leggings that I'd worn in that day. I'd brought in a gray pencil skirt and a green blouse. It was something simple, not too sexy or too sweet. It said, "I wanna look good but I don't want you to think we're fucking tonight." You had to send the right message with your outfit.

"Where you headed tonight?" asked Edmonds, one of my fellow newbies. She'd been on the job for a few weeks longer than I had but she still got treated the same as me. She was a cool chick. She and I usually kept it light when we spoke, not really knowing too much about one another yet. "That skirt is nice. Where'd you get it?"

"Thanks," I said as I closed my locker and

grabbed my bag. "One of them Instagram boutiques. I can show you which one tomorrow if you want. I'm in a rush." I smiled at her.

"Ok, no problem. Have fun girl. I hope he's funny," she said. She winked at me and I smiled again before walking off and heading out the door.

Of course some of the guys heckled me as I walked out. They whistled and catcalled, typical male shit but I kept it all in stride and just gave them the finger and a smile. I was learning what it meant to be a part of their world so I knew the rules.

I headed to my car to drop my bag off. Thankfully the place that Reggie had chosen was in walking distance of my precinct. I kept checking my phone to see if he'd texted or called. I don't know why but I was expecting him to say that he was gonna be late or something like that.

I was about to cross the street when someone caught my attention off to my left. Someone had just walked passed me and it looked like that dude Young. I didn't wanna look thirsty if it was him so I didn't move but two seconds later, that shit went out the window. I almost broke my neck turning it to see if it was him. The dude wasn't there though. I turned around to look further down the block but I didn't see anyone that looked like him.

Was I bugging? Had my mind been playing tricks on me? I know that it was only out of my peripheral vision but I knew that I'd *seen* him, even if it was quick and out the corner of my eyes. I just kept on walking, deciding to shrug off my sighing as nothing but a trick of the light.

I got to the place right on time. Reggie was just walking up as I was. I walked up to him and his eyes quickly glanced my over from head to toe before he looked me in my eyes. He leaned in and wrapped an arm around me, pulling me closer to him.

"How are you?" he asked. "You look good."

"Thanks," I said. "You do too." Reggie was dressed in a pair of fitted jeans, brown boots, and a checkered patterned shirt. It was a simple look, something very first date like. It wasn't my usual flavor for a guy but Reggie wore it well. He smelled good too so he was definitely earning points in my book.

We headed into the place and got a table for

two. We'd lucked out and still had an hour of Happy Hour left. The waitress told us what the specials were and left us alone to think about our drinks. I looked down at the menu. There were so many drinks listed that it was messing up my choice making process.

The place a typical bar with the usual Mexican flare to it, flags, sombreros, cactus, you know, the type of shit that means Mexican to Americans. It was nice and big though and it smelled amazing. I couldn't see the kitchen but I could smell it and every scent in the air made my mouth water.

"Have you been here before?" I asked.

"Yeah, my coworkers and I have come here after work a couple of times. The drinks are good," Reggie said.

"What are you gonna get?" I asked.

"A margarita," he said.

I thought for a moment. "Yeah, sounds good. I'll get one too. You'd have to work hard to mess up a margarita." The waitress came back over and took our drink orders, leaving us alone.

"So, tell me about yourself," Reggie said. His hazel eyes were dancing in the light.

"What do you want to know?" I asked. I actually kind of hated it when people said that to me. If it wasn't a job interview, you needed to be more specific about your questions.

"Anything," Reggie said.

I wished that the waitress had brought the drinks over already but I just smiled. "I'm 23 years old, and I'm a born and raised New Yorker. What about you?"

"I'm actually not from the city," he said.

"Where are you from?" I asked.

"Ithaca, New York," he said. "Lived at home my whole life until I went to college."

"Cornell University, in Ithaca," he said. "But I've always want to live in New York City. My parents are both from here but they moved when they got pregnant with me. They never wanted to raise their kids in the city.'"

"That makes sense. I don't know if I want to raise mine here either," I said. "What about New York made you want to come here so bad?"

Reggie seemed to light up then. "Are you kidding me? This place is amazing. There's just so much culture here. It's not like this in Ithaca.

We're 4 hours away but it feels like a different world."

"I know what you mean," I said. "I feel the same way when I go visit my grandma in New Rochelle."

Reggie smiled. "Did she like her gift?"

"You remembered," I smiled as the waitress brought our drinks over. "Yeah, she loved the hat. I don't know if she's worn it yet."

"That was really sweet of you," Reggie said. "So, tell me more about you. I been talking about me. What do you do for fun? Where you work at?"

"I'm a cop, new to the job though. No war stories over here," I said. I'd figured out that when people heard you were a cop, they wanted to hear all about your most gruesome stories and stuff. Unless Reggie wanted to hear about Brantwell's sweat, I had nothing for him. "For fun, I just like to have fun. I'm a bar or club kind of girl. I also work out and stuff too. I'm big on running."

Reggie licked his lips. "Yeah, you have nice legs," he flirted with me.

"Thanks," I said.

"Maybe we can go for a run together some-
time," he said.

"I'd like that," I smiled.

Reggie and I enjoyed one another's
company for almost two hours. It was great
because he knew how to talk in person, just like
he had on the phone. He told me all about his
job as an accountant. He was single and open to
a relationship with the right person but made it
clear that he wasn't pressed.

Reggie and I got along well because he was
on the same page as me. I like to eat and I loved
food so when he suggested that we just try a
bunch of dishes on the menu, I was with it.

We ended the night off with a sweet kiss. I
told him that I was walking back to my car and
he walked with me. He was taking a cab but
before he walked off, he'd pulled me in close to
him and we had a great kiss.

I was in the car driving home with the radio
on. Mary J. Blige had just come out with a new
album so they were playing it. Mary was going
through a lot so she was making some of her
best music.

I was reflecting on the date with Reggie as I
headed home. Had I enjoyed myself? Yes. Did I

see a future with Reggie? No. I don't know what it is but it just didn't connect on my end. I've always been good at reading people and I could tell that he was into me but the feeling wasn't mutual. Don't get me wrong, Reggie was a great guy and everything. He was handsome, smart, funny, pretty much the whole package but for some reason I just wasn't feeling him like that.

I wasn't about to be stupid about it though. Just because *I* knew I wasn't feeling Reggie didn't mean that Reggie needed to know that. I was gonna add him to my rotation. I wasn't about to let a dude like that go. Who knows what the future holds?

CHAPTER 5

"Bitch, you up?" Jessica asked.

I was in my bed, laying on my side. My phone started ringing in my sleep and I'd just answered it and put it on my face. I was in the middle of a dream. I was about to get married but I didn't know to who. The aisle was too long for me to see who was at the end.

"What time is it?" I asked. I was halfway asleep. It was Saturday morning, at least that's when I thought it was. I glanced out the window and saw that it was dark still.

"5:03 in the morning," she said, her voice full of life. Jessica was one of my closest friends and had been for years. She wasn't my best friend but we were close as hell. . She and I'd met one another in junior high. We were in the same class and had just stayed cool ever since, even when we didn't go to the same high schools. Jessica had become a flight attendant and she loved it. She'd been at it for a little over two years and really enjoyed doing it.

"Bye," I said. My voice was still full of sleep. "You can't be serious, Jess. I told you about these early calls before."

"Don't hang up on me! I'm gonna be in New York," she said. Jessica had was from New York and wanted to live here but when the airline hired her, they told her that there was only a chance that she'd be in New York. Her home base was in Houston, Texas, so she lived there.

"For how long?" I asked. Jessica was always in New York, just like she was always in places all over the world. I liked that she got to do something she'd always wanted to do. Not to mention that whenever she went places she always sent me and some of our friend post-cards. It was cool to get them from all over the world.

"27 hours bitch!" she yelled. If I had the energy I would have moved the phone but I just rolled my eyes and then closed them. I hoped that I'd be able to get back to sleep for a couple more hours. "That means I'm with the shits! Where we going? I'm trying to get out and see the city. You know I'm not in New York often."

"When do you get here?" I asked. Going out with Jessica was always mad fun. She'd been all around the world so her ideas of fun could be a little out there but I just went with her, always knowing that I'd have a good time.

"I'll be there later on today," she said. I could hear the excitement in her voice.

"Alright, sounds like a plan," I said with a yawn. "Look, hit me up when you're here and we can go out."

"Ok, cool," she said. "How's your cousin Shante? You wanna invite her out?"

"I been so busy I haven't even spoken to her. Yeah, I'll hit her up in a little bit," I said.

"Just call her on three way," Jessica said.

"Jess, the sun ain't even up. Everybody ain't on world time like you," I said with a chuckle.

"You're right," she said. "I'll hit you up later."

After Jessica and I got off the phone, I went back to sleep. A couple of hours later I got up feeling very refreshed. I went for a run and then came back in a made a healthy breakfast of egg whites and whole wheat toast. It wasn't ideal but I was trying to lose weight and build muscle.

I cleaned up my crib and really chilled out. I had a long conversation with my mother and she was being nosey as usual, asking all about my date with Reggie. I told her about it but left out the fact that we didn't really have chemistry. It wasn't a secret or anything but my mother could sometimes do a lot and I didn't need to hear her mouth. I knew that in her head, Reggie was the kind of guy I should get with.

A little before 5, Jessica showed up. She'd just arrived at JFK and had taken a cab straight to my house.

Jessica walked in like her usual self, over the top as usual. Her bag was rolling behind her as she walked in and she dropped it to the floor as she walked over to me. The two of us grabbed each other up, holding tightly. It was so nice to see her.

We broke our hug and stepped back, each of us taking one another in. Jessica was a good looking girl. She had brown skin and dark brown hair that was thick. She wore it naturally, but because of work she just wore wigs that were the same color. Jessica had always been a thick girl, big thighs, ass, hips, everything. She'd always had a little pudgy stomach too but she never did anything to get rid of it. She'd always say that as long as it never got bigger she was fine and I guess she worked out to keep it that way.

"You look good girl," she said to me. Her light brown eyes danced as she looked me over.

"So do you," I said. I picked up her bag and closed and locked my front door. We headed into my spacious living room and sat down on my couch. "So, where you off to next?"

"Amsterdam," she announced with a smile. "I was there last month too. It was cool. You know I wish I would've been able to smoke though."

I scoffed. "Girl! You telling me? I ain't about to mess up my job with that though," I said.

"Yes, that's right. Mrs. Officer and all that. How's it been going?" Jessica asked. "You know I'm really proud of you, right Tae? I'm glad you're out here grinding like this."

"Thanks Jess, I appreciate it," I said. "It's been going good. I like it so far. It's not what I thought it would be but that might be for the best."

"It's crazy that you're a cop, you of all people," she said. "You're just so damn bubbly and shit. You're more cheerleader than cop."

"'I know, right?" I said. "I can't front, I was just as surprised as everyone else was when I graduated but I made it through. It wasn't easy but I'm here."

"I really am proud of you," Jessica said.

"I appreciate it," I said. "It means a lot to me."

"No problem. We've come a long way from those two little girls with all the bow bow's and stuff in our hair, huh?" Jessica asked with a laugh.

"Thankfully," I said.

"What are your coworkers like? Are cops the way they are on TV?" she asked. She was serious too.

"They're cool," I said. "I'm still getting to know people though. There's a lot of names and a lot of faces. All of these shifts coming in and out all the time."

"I know how that can be," she said. Jessica's work as a flight attendant always had her working with different pilots and stuff. She used to tell me that it was nice to run into some of the same people whenever she could. "Are any of them cute?"

"Who? The guys I work with?" I asked with a laugh. The look on her face said she was dead serious though. "I haven't seen any, yet. But I'll be on the lookout." I winked at her and she smiled.

Jessica and I spent more time catching up with one another. She was always on the go because of her job so we didn't ever really get a chance to chop it up. She was excited to go out. I'd called my cousin Shante and she was down to go out as well. I was excited too because it had been a while since I'd been out and even longer since I'd chilled with either of them.

At a little after seven, Shante got to the house. My cousin Shante and I were mad cool growing up since we were so close to one another in age. She and I still spoke frequently as adults and we tried to hang out as often as we could but it had been a couple of weeks since we'd chilled so it was nice to see her.

Once Shante was there, that was it. We put on some music, poured some drinks and started getting dressed. I had a bottle of vodka in the house and Shante brought over some prosecco. I stashed the prosecco in the fridge and made us three screwdrivers—vodka and orange juice. I also put in some peach schnapps and pineapple juice; that was so the drinks would be strong but the liquor's taste would be hidden.

"What you gonna wear?" Shante asked me. "You've already changed twice, girl. You need help."

"Put this on," Jessica said. She was only partially dressed herself but she was holding out a dress of mine from a hanger for me to put on.

"Nah," I shook my head. "Not that one."

"Why?" Shante asked. She took the hanger from Jessica and held it up. It was a gray lace dress with a cinched waist and an open back. It also gripped the hell out of my body and made me look fat.

"I look big as hell in that," I said. She extended her arm and held the dress up to me.

"It looks like you should be fine," she said. "At least just try it on." I looked to Jessica for support but she just told me to try it on too.

I rolled my eyes and and went to try it on. I

came back out a couple of minutes later with the dress on. "Happy?" I asked.

"You gotta wear that! Bitch you look like everything! I'm jealous. It looks like you had your butt done," Jessica said. Don't you know she had the nerve to actually pout.

"What? Y'all bugging. I'm not wearing this," I said. I wasn't feeling as comfortable as I would have liked.

"Bitch did you even look at yourself? You better wear that dress," Shante said.

I walked over to the mirror in the room and stood in front of it. I had to admit that the dress didn't look as bad as it used to. It was a lot tighter than things I normally wore and maybe that was what threw me off about it. I turned to the side and looked at myself. My ass *did* look nice.

"She likes it," Shante said from behind me with a laugh. Jessica and I joined in.

A little after ten we ended up leaving the house to head to the spot that Shante told us about. We'd been in the house talking so much and singing our hearts out to so many songs that we didn't even really drink. None of the three of us had finished our drinks and we were in a rush to go so we just decided to drink at the club.

Roxie's was some spot that I'd heard of a couple of times. It was in Midtown and apparently had a nice crowd that was usually mixed but tended to be more of the Hip Hop crowd. I was glad too. I needed to hear some good music and turn up with my girls. It had been so long since we'd been around one another and I really wanted to enjoy it.

We hopped out of our cab and didn't see a crowd of people outside. We didn't let that stop us though. We headed inside after the bouncer checked us. I knew that the night was gonna be something special because as quiet as the place seemed from the outside, it *definitely* wasn't like that inside. We didn't even walk inside the club, the DJ was playing all the tunes and the three of us danced our way in.

The club was nicer on the inside. It had huge ceilings with two huge chandeliers and a some mini disco balls hanging from the ceiling. All of the decor was red or black. There were small tables and bigger VIP sections.

Roxie's was crowded inside. I guess that a lot of people had our same mindset about getting there early. We made our way around the club, seeing who was inside and also looking for a table. After walking around for a couple of minutes we found one and grabbed it. Thankfully we wouldn't have to buy bottles as long as we kept getting drinks, even though I figured we'd probably end up getting one anyway.

We ordered a couple of drinks and just started to let loose. I was feeling sexy and confident that night. I had on the gray dress with black heels that made me look taller. I was gonna wear my hair down but the girls said that I should put it up, so I wore it in a high bun. I didn't normally wear makeup but I'd let Jessica do a really natural look.

"I like this DJ!" Shante said. Our drinks had just come and we were sipping them and it looked like we'd be needing another round. Yeah, a bottle or two was definitely in the future for us.

We spent the next half hour or so really getting into our groove. The DJ was going in and playing all the stuff that we wanted to hear. I was hype as hell. Jessica was of course on a 10, that's just who she was. Shante was letting loose too. Both of them had danced with a guy or two. I'd had a couple of them approach me but I'd just been dancing by myself at the table for the most part.

"What you waiting for?" Shante asked. She'd just come back over from dancing with some guy. She looked a little sweaty but her makeup was still perfect.

I opened my mouth to answer but the DJ started shouting out that he was gonna play some new Nicki Minaj song. It came on and the crowd went crazy. The beat was bonkers, all the bass and it was perfect to twerk to.

In that moment I just wanted to dance. I told Shante I'd be back and headed to the dance floor. I walked around for a little bit until I saw a guy that I thought was cute. He was light skinned with jet black hair and a goatee. He was giving me the eye so I walked up to him and asked him if he wanted to dance. It wasn't my normal thing but I was trying to get outside of my normal self. He smiled and said yeah. I could tell he was happy.

The guy and I danced for the whole song. I was really feeling the song so it made it easy for me to really just go off to it. I hadn't heard it before but the beat was so catchy that I just kept on movin'. The dude I was dancing with was doing his best to keep up with me. When the song ended, I dismissed him. I wasn't feeling him. He was trying to keep up with me but wasn't really succeeding and nothing was worse than a guy who couldn't dance.

You know how sometimes you can be at a club and it's empty one minute and full the next? Somehow in the time that it had taken me to dance and dismiss old boy, the club had become packed as hell. I took a deep breath, just thinking about how aggravating it was about to be to get myself all the way to the other side of the club. I hated pushing past people and Lord knows that some of them stink.

I decided that I could just hang out for a minute by myself. The next song came on and I danced by myself. I was really feeling it.

I hadn't noticed it but a couple of people had been watching me dance and I recognized one of their faces. Young, the criminal from the precinct, was in the club and looked smooth as hell in all black. His black jeans were up on his waist and showed off a designer belt. He was wearing a black V-neck t-shirt with a gold cross hanging on his neck. His body looked solid as hell, like he'd just come from working out or something.

I couldn't take my eyes off of him. The song had switched again, this time something with a little reggae beat. I watched as he danced by himself in a way that was just...cool. It was effortless, the way he moved was like he knew the beats before he heard them. He was magnetic and I was being pulled in.

I made my way over to him and we didn't say anything. We didn't need to. His body caught my rhythm and mine caught his. The two of us grinded on one another for three songs straight. Back to front, front to back. We were pressed dick to ass and then I turned around and he put his hands on the small of my back. He lowered himself down to me and I watched the lights of the club bounce off of his chocolate skin. I took a deep breath of his cologne. It smelled kind of like citrus.

The weirdest thing about the entire exchange with Young was that neither of us spoke. We said a lot to one another but not with words. When the three songs were over it was almost like we just knew we'd danced enough. I turned around to him. He was looking down at me and then we just separated. I went back over to Shante and Jessica and he disappeared just as mysteriously as he'd appeared in the first place.

I didn't realize how long I'd been gone but the looks on their faces definitely told me it was too long. I plopped down on the small couch next to Jessica.

"You remembered we were here, huh?" Jessica asked. She busted out laughing though. She couldn't be serious if she wanted to. "How was your dance?"

"Which one?" I asked with a laugh. I put up my hand and she high fived it.

"I hear that!" Jessica said. "I had a couple too."

Shante was looking at me with a little confusion. "What?" I asked.

"Do you know what that was?" She asked. She had a serious look on her face.

"Who?" I asked. I was trying my hardest to play it off. We'd each had a couple of drinks so paying dumb wasn't really a problem. I knew she had to be talking about Young though.

"That tall dude," Shante said. "His name is Young."

"Who's he?" Jessica asked.

"Somebody that Tae, a new member of the NYPD, should stay away from," Shante said loudly over the music. "He's into a little bit of everything I hear. He's a gang leader."

"Really? He ain't look like a gang leader. And he damn sure ain't dance like one," I said. I thought about the dance and wanted to do it all over again.

"Well he is," Shante said, snapping me from my thoughts. "From what I hear he's smooth as hell with the ladies and has their men in check. He's knee deep in some shady shit and you need to stay away from him, Tae."

Shante was giving me a look that let me know how serious she was. The problem was that the more she spoke, the more intrigued I found myself. I wanted to know more about this man that was so feared and ruthless but still so charming and seemingly nice. I knew Shante had my best intentions in mind but I was thinking about taking a walk on the wild side...if I got a chance, that was. I wasn't about to go risking my career or anything to go chasing after behind some dude just because I thought he was cute.

"I hear you," I said. "Thanks for looking out

for me." She smiled at me. I reached down into the bucket that was halfway full with melted ice and grabbed the bottle of champagne. "We need to finish this!"

We stayed at the club for a little while longer before the three of us headed back to my house. It wasn't too late when we got in so we kicked it like we did when we were younger and just had a sleepover. We wrapped our hair, put on pajamas, opened wine and just talked and laughed.

Of course we spoke about men and relationships. I told the girls about my date with Reggie because I wanted to get their opinions on it. I knew that sometimes I could be a little quick to judge so I made sure to tell them every detail so that they could judge me fairly. I wanted to know if I was being picky by wanting to have chemistry with a guy as opposed to just liking him because he seemed to have it together.

Of course neither of them had been much in the way of help. Jessica told me that chemistry was the way to go. "If there's no spark, there's no flame," she said. I had to admit that she had a point.

Shante had made a case for the fact that he was a nice guy who probably had a good future ahead of him. She said that even if we didn't have chemistry at first, Reggie represented stability which was something I'd need in my new life as an officer.

The night had been very impromptu but we got it together. It felt good to reunite with my girls. I made sure to tell Jessica that I was glad that she suggested the night out. It was exactly what each of us needed. I didn't admit it out loud but I was also glad that the night had given me another chance to Young again. When I finally did go to sleep, I was wondering when I'd have the chance to see him again.

CHAPTER 6

MONDAY MORNING CAME AROUND and hit me like a ton of bricks. Before I knew it my ass was back at work, still tired from the weekend. Staying up into Sunday had definitely messed up my sleep for Monday and I'd been trying to correct it. Needless to say that I was a little off. I still got there on time and listened intently while they went over the numbers and assignments for the day in the morning briefing, among other things.

There was some paperwork that I needed to take care of so I'd brought it into the briefing with me. It was nothing much, just some stuff for HR and some paperwork for a case that I'd caught with Brantwell. When the briefing was over I kneeled down to grab the large envelope and stack of stapled papers that I'd brought with me. The chairs in the room were the old school kind with baskets underneath to store your things and a place for you to lean on. Looking down at the papers, I noticed something strange. There was something there that wasn't there before. Folded on top of the envelope was a piece of yellow legal paper. It wasn't mine, I knew that for sure. I hadn't seen it before. I unfolded it and saw that there were some words written on it.

Call Young was written and beneath that was a telephone number. I looked around, trying to see who could have put the piece of paper there but half the room had cleared out. The thing that had me bugging out was the fact that the briefing room was closed to anyone but police. No civilians or criminals were allowed in unless it was under special circumstances. That meant that Young had at least one person working for him in the precinct and I figured there had to be more. No wonder he was so confident he'd get out that day.

Young was on my mind all day long. I was trying to focus on doing what I was doing, especially since I'd been getting the chance to get out a little more and do some real work. I just couldn't keep my mind off of the mysterious man.

Young wasn't just cute, he was handsome. God had taken time piecing that man together bit by bit. I hadn't spoken a word to him yet and I found him charismatic and alluring, Hearing so many different stories about him made me want to know more about him.

I wasn't about to go falling head over heels though. I wasn't stupid and I knew that all of the same things that made Young mysterious were the exact same things that I needed to stay my ass away from. Shante really hadn't told me much that I didn't know about Young from the briefing but I was starting to think I knew enough. If I decided to mess with him and it blew up in my face, it could mean the end of my career before it had a chance to get started for real.

I thought about it a lot during the day and finally made a decision: it wasn't gonna be up to me. I'd leave it up to Young. I decided to at least have a conversation with him. I felt like I owed him at least that much since he'd gone through all the trouble of contacting me at work. The way the conversation went would determine what would happen next. I might end up talking to him and not even liking him anymore. There could be no real chemistry with him just like Reggie.

Some people might have thought I was bugging out, which was why I didn't tell anyone what I was doing. After work I drove to a Duane Reade and bought a disposable cell phone. There was no way in hell I was about to call him from my actual number. I didn't know if his phone was tapped or something like that so I didn't want to risk it.

Once I got in the house I dropped my bags and plopped down on the couch. I activated the phone after taking it out the box. I took a deep breath and dialed Young's number. Before it could ring I hung up the phone.

I stood up and took the phone with me into my bedroom. I sat on the edge of the bed trying to get my feelings together. I was nervous, excited, exhilarated, curious, just the full range of emotions. I was trying to get control of myself. I felt like a little kid or something. It got so bad that I had to stand up and start pacing the floor. I didn't know if I was trying to talk myself down or hype myself up. I tried as hard as i could to stop myself from thinking about making the call but I couldn't. I took it as a sign that I needed to stop playing around and just call.

I sat back down on the edge of the bed and decided to call right then and there. I took a deep breath and pressed the button to call him back. The call connected and it started to ring. My heart was beating fast and I looked up at the ceiling in disbelief. I couldn't believe that I was doing this.

"Yo, who's this?" Young's deep voice snapped me from my thoughts and made my heart skip a beat. He sounded so sexy on the phone.

"Hello?" I said.

"Oh shit," he said. "Is this Mrs. Officer?" I could tell that he was smiling through the phone.

"It's Tae," I corrected him. "But I think you already knew that. I got your message, obviously."

"I'm surprised you called," Young said.

"Me too," I admitted. I was nervous being

on the phone with him and it had nothing to do with what he did for a living. It was the typical feeling someone had when they spoke to a person they were interested in for the first time.

"I ain't think you'd snitch or anything like that when you got my message, but I wasn't expecting you to hit me up so soon," he said. "It's cool though. How was your day?"

Young was talking to me like we were old friends and instead of feeling awkward, I went with it. "It was alright. I just worked."

"How was work?" Young asked. It was weird to me that he was being so sincere. I was even more surprised when I told him all about my day and he just listened instead of interrupting. When he did speak, he asked insightful questions that let me know he'd actually been paying attention to me.

For more than twenty minutes, Young and I sat on the phone with another and talked about everything under the sun. By the time the call was over I knew that I had only one option: I had to see where it would go with him. Yes, on paper Young might have been a criminal. He might have been described as violent and dangerous by some but there was none of that on the phone.

He was smart and funny. He kept the conversation going seamlessly and made me laugh a couple of times. Young was also "woke" too. We'd briefly talked about politics and how the two of us were on different sides of the track but still making it work. I had to admit that it was refreshing to talk to someone who could talk about so many topics.

While we were on the phone, we both decided that we wanted to get to know another better in person. The problem was that we both kept thinking about it but couldn't come up with a free and clear way for the two of us to go out on a date. I wasn't involved in the investigation with him so I couldn't say for sure whether or not people were watching him but I didn't want to risk it. I just wanted it to be something low key and he was feeling the same thing.

"You could just come to my crib," Young joked.

"You're real funny," I said with a smile. I was feeling him and didn't mind talking to him for as long as he wanted to be on the phone.

"Nah, but I'm dead serious about seeing you, Mrs. Officer," he said.

"You know my name is Tae, right?" I asked.

"I know a lot about you," Young said in his own mysterious way. "How else you think I got you that message?"

"You're something else," I said. "And I do wanna hear all about how you got that message to me. It was real slick."

Young laughed. It was a deep but quick one but I joined in for a little bit. "All in due time. I can't tell you all my secrets. You work for the other side."

I knew that he'd been joking but the fact that I was a police officer and he was a criminal seemed to hang over our entire conversation. We tried to come up with ways to meet one another but couldn't, neither of us really mentioning the elephant in the room.

"But we can worry about that later though. I gotta go run. I got some stuff to handle," he said.

"Oh, ok," I said. I was surprised because I was actually a little disappointed that he wanted to get off the phone. I was actually enjoying the conversation with him. "No problem. You have my number now so you can hit me up if you want to."

"And I will," he said in a way that let me know he was serious. "I'll holla at you later."

"Later," I said. I pressed the button to end the call.

I dropped the phone on the bed and then turned and started screaming into my pillow. I kicked my legs into the air and flung my feet back and forth. I was so hype! My body felt like it was on fire. I felt like I was back in high school or something. I felt like a teenager sneaking behind my parents back or something. It was definitely forbidden but that was making it all the more tempting.

I stopped making all the noise because I heard something coming from the living room. I got quiet and heard the sound of my *real* phone ringing. I got up and ran to answer it, getting to it right before it went to voicemail.

"Hello?" I answered the phone. I'd picked it up so quick that I didn't even have a chance to look at who it was.

"What's up, Tae? It's Reggie," he said.

I sat down on the couch. "Hey, how are you?" I asked. I couldn't lie; I wished I would have just let it go to voicemail. I was still on my high from my conversation with Young and even though Reggie was cool, he wasn't doing for me what Young was doing.

"I'm good. What are you up to?" he asked.

"Nothing much, just relaxing after a long day," I said. "How about you?"

"Same thing. I'd been thinking about you since we went out the other night so I decided to hit you up and see if you wanted to go out again," he said.

"Sure, what'd you have in mind?" I asked. I tried to sound enthused. I remembered that I told myself that I wasn't going to dismiss Reggie yet.

"I was thinking dinner," he said. "How about Saturday night?"

"I'm free," I said.

"Ok, sounds great. If you have a place in mind, let me know. If not then I'll pick," he said. He sounded excited. I'm glad one of us was.

"Alright, sounds good," I said. I took a deep breath. "I'm about to go take a shower and then lay down so I'll hit you up later."

"Oh," he sounded disappointed. "No problem. Have a good night."

"You too," I said.

When Reggie and I got off the phone, I was almost completely sure that there were no romantic feelings at all between us. He might not have known it but I *definitely* did. There just wasn't a spark between us, at least not romantically. I would have been kidding myself if I thought that we could be friends. Being friend-zoned was awkward, unless it happened naturally and something told me that it wasn't about to be that.

Before I got into bed and laid down I climbed into the shower just like I said I would to Reggie. While I was in there I couldn't help but think about how funny it was the way that life worked out sometimes. Reggie was the guy that I didn't want and he was readily available when I wanted to meet up with him. Young was the guy I really wanted to see but that would be damn near impossible because of who we were. If only they could have switched places or something.

CHAPTER 7

SATURDAY ROLLED AROUND after a long work week and I couldn't have been happier for it. Going in to work day in and day out was good because it took care of the bills but I definitely felt as though I'd earned a break and that day I planned on enjoying it and making the most out of the weekend. I had a date later with Reggie that I planned on keeping but in the meantime I wanted to take myself out and do something nice.

The world that I worked in left me no time to just be a girl. I worked around men all day long and had to deal with that. I'd had a couple of conversations with some of the female officers who'd been around for a while. They made it clear that though things were progressing, this was still a very male dominated world for the most part. One of them said that even though no one said it, there was a lot of pressure on the women to "just be one of the boys" as she put it.

Professionally speaking it was something that I could deal with. As long as you worked for someone else, you had to take into account what they wanted and how they did things. Outside of that was your time to be what you wanted and on that particular Saturday all I wanted to do was let someone else take care of me for a change. I hadn't planned it out but I knew that I wanted to go get my nails and hair done and maybe a massage on top of that. I could also have done some shopping because retail therapy was the only kind that I needed.

I stayed in bed until almost 9AM which was late for me. I wished I could have slept longer but my body was just too used to getting up early. I was thinking of taking myself out for breakfast but I was already planning on spending enough as is with all the other stuff I planned on doing. I ended up just making myself some breakfast: oatmeal with berries and some water, nothing fancy.

After I ate, I took a shower and got dressed. I didn't know how long I'd be out so I kept it cute and casual in a pair of medium blue jeans, sneakers, and a black shirt. It was simple and to the point.

I decided to go and get my nails done first. Before I starting working as a police officer, I definitely would have just gone to my local hood spot and get my nails done. It was nothing to go run to Ms. Julie and let her hook me up. I was making more money though I decided to try out another place instead.

Nail Art in Harlem was one of the newest businesses around but it had made a name for itself for being so upscale, and the fact that it was black owned. You paid more there then you did at the regular salon but they did more for you, so it balanced out. Nail Art would play music softly in the background while they did your hands and feet. You could also order girly cocktails and other things while you were getting services. The place itself was nicely decorated and they were really nice too. I guess money made a difference.

I had to wait a couple of minutes for someone to come over to me but once they did they escorted me to a chair where I sat. The guy about to do my feet asked me if I wanted something to drink before he started. Another woman came over and brought me a mimosa after I ordered it.

The guy doing my feet was annoyed with me in a couple of minutes. He hadn't said anything about it though. I could just tell. He was doing a really good job on my feet but the problem was that I was ticklish. He'd move my feet and I was start to giggle. I was trying not to but it just tickled so much. I had to just stare up at the ceiling to help myself. I knew I was acting like a big kid but I couldn't help it.

After a couple of minutes of cutting, rubbing, and massaging my feet, the guy finally stopped. He placed both of my feet into a warm bath and told me to just sit a couple of minutes and relax. I looked down at the water and noticed that it had a green tint to it. I wasn't sure of what they put into the water but I was feeling stress free. I felt like all the bullshit and stress that had been annoying me or on my mind was leaving my body and I was so thankful for that.

I got a French manicure done next. The

same guy did my hands and I didn't laugh this time, even though it tickled when he massaged them too. My nails needed to dry so the guy sat me at one of the stations in front of a window. I put my nails into the machine and stared out the window, doing some people watching.

When I was younger I'd always people watch from my windows. I used to have a little game where I'd make up a whole story about a person—who they were and where they were headed. I still did it every now and then.

I glanced down at my nails to see if they were dry. They weren't so I put them back under the warm air of the machine. When I looked back up out the window, I saw someone walk by dressed in a gray sweat suit and a pair of Jordans. I could have sworn it was Young, so much that I even stood up and tried to get a better look at him as he left my view.

If it was him, I'd never know now. The tall figure was long gone, down the block. I thought that I had to be bugging out after a while. It didn't make any sense. Could I *really* be seeing Young everywhere like that? It didn't make any sense. I couldn't have been mistaking him that often, could I?

I was making progress with my pampering. Now that my nails had been done, my next destination was the salon. My girl Taleshia was gonna hook me up. I'd been going to her for years. When she moved shops, so did I. She'd seen me through a bunch of hairstyles so I really trusted her with my hair.

It was a Saturday afternoon so of course the shop was full. Normally I would have tried to be one of the first ones there but I was just taking my time that day. I'd texted Taleshia to let her know around what time to expect me. She told me it was cool and gave me a little fifteen minute window that I could get in between. She also told me that if I didn't get there during that time that I might as well just wait until Monday. Needless to say that I was in a hurry.

I got to the shop with time to spare. I said my greetings to the people that I knew and headed straight to Taleshia. She looked like she was taking a break, sitting in her chair relaxing. Taleshia's caramel colored skin and exotic features made her a big hit with the guys. She and I were cool so sometimes we spoke and she'd tell me about the guys that tried to talk to her when she went out.

"Wassup boo?" Taleshia asked as she stood up to free the chair. I walked up to her and hugged her and kissed her on the cheek.

"How you doing?" I asked her.

"Can't complain. It's been busy as hell in here," she said. I could see that too. The shop was packed with people. There was no place to sit. Pretty much every station was full of people at various stages of getting their hair done. I was glad that Taleshia had space for me.

"I can see," I said as I put my stuff down and took a seat in the chair. Taleshia put the apron over me and got started. My hair was naturally curly but I wanted her to give me bigger curls and more body. I didn't have to go into much detail because Taleshia pretty much knew how I wanted it.

The conversations that happened inside of a beauty salon on a Saturday could be about anything. The topics ranged but they typically stayed revolving around the same thing in many forms: men. That particular Saturday they were talking about how long a woman should wait to sleep with a man after the first date. I didn't plan on joining in the conversation but I definitely listened to every word.

"It don't matter," said this one girl named Simone. "I slept with James on the first date and he and I were together for three years."

"That's true," said someone else.

"But Simone, ain't you go out with some nigga last week who ain't call you back?" Someone else asked with a laugh. Simone looked a little annoyed but she kept on going.

"My point is this: if a guy really likes you, it don't matter when y'all sleep together," Simone said.

I nodded my head. She had a point. I didn't know if I believed in fate and all that but I did think that if you were meant to be with someone that you'd find a way to do it. It didn't matter about when you slept with them.

"Oh please," said another girl. "That sounds nice and all but y'all are acting like we not dealing with these niggas who ain't got no sense. They got a high set of standards, even if they don't bring shit to the table. If you give the pussy up too fast, you're a thot. If you take too long, you're stuck up. Ain't no way *I'm* giving up the pussy on the first date."

She got a lot of approval for that. As time went on, the debate went back and forth with people giving opinions on both sides. After a couple of hours, Taleshia had finished my hair. She spun me around into the mirror and I had to admit that she'd really hooked me up. I was gushing over my new hairdo as I left the shop and headed downtown to do some shopping.

I made my way into a bunch of stores. I was looking for a new pair of shoes and a dress but if I saw some other cute things, I wouldn't just leave them. I pretty much knew which stores I wanted to go to because I'd been eyeing the stuff for a while. I headed inside and tried the dress on and was happy to find that it fit just the way I wanted it to. I bought it and the shoes that I wanted and as I was heading home to get ready for my date with Reggie later, I couldn't help but think about how good the day had been. I'd really taken time out for myself and it felt great. I knew every Saturday couldn't be like that but I at least wanted to do it once a month. I was fine with doing it alone too.

I got home and chilled out for a little bit before I started getting ready. I was hanging out on the couch, relaxing after having been out all day when my mind drifted to Young. It started off with me thinking about that guy from earlier that might or might not have been him and then from there I just couldn't stop thinking about him. I don't know what it was about him that made him seem so magnetic but I really liked it. It was thinking about him so much that I even thought about cancelling my date with Reggie. In the end I decided not to.

I got up and started getting ready. I showered, did my makeup, and got dressed. Reggie had hit me up to tell me the place for our second date. I tried to think of a way to seem more interested than I was, but it wasn't working.

I showed up at the restaurant on time and so did he. He did look good in his outfit, I'd give him that much. The date itself went fine. We talked. We laughed. But once again I just didn't feel any chemistry. I was hoping that it would be better the second time around but it was just more of the same.

Once we'd paid up and headed out of the restaurant, we both lingered to talk to one another. Reggie grabbed my hand and we started to walk down the block headed nowhere in particular.

"I really enjoyed myself. How about you?" he asked.

I knew that it was probably going to hurt his feelings but I needed to be as honest as possible. I wasn't feeling Reggie and I knew it for sure then. "I don't wanna make this awkward or anything like that, but I'm just not sure this is gonna work out. I think you're a great guy. You're nice and funny, but I don't really feel a connection," I said. We'd stopped walking and I was making sure to look him in the eyes so he knew I was serious.

Reggie looked shocked. His eyes got wide and then they narrowed. I could see something in his eyes and it looked like anger. It was clear that he hadn't been expecting me to say it. I knew that it had to be rough for him but it had to be said. The alternative was that we both kept wasting our time and I definitely wasn't about to do that.

"Well since you feel that way, have a nice life!" Reggie snapped at me. He stormed off, heading down the block and turning the corner. I knew he had to be pissed off but I was doing him a favor. I knew that it wasn't going anywhere.

I was standing there all dressed up with nothing to do. I'd worn the new outfit out with Reggie and had expected to be tired after being out all day but I wasn't. It was a little after 11 and the night was still young.

Watching Reggie walk off had triggered something in me. I realized that I needed to get my shit together and figure out what the hell was going on with me and Young. Now I was really distraction free, not talking to Reggie. A thought came to my mind and I decided to act on it, quickly. I pulled that disposable phone out of my bag and dialed the only number that it had ever called.

"Wassup Mrs. Officer?" Young answered the phone in a familiar voice.

"Are you busy right now?" I asked. I could hear people talking in his background but I wasn't sure about what.

"A little bit but nothing crazy. Why? You good?" he asked. He sounded a little concerned. I thought it was cute.

"Everything's fine," I said. "I was just seeing if you wanted to go out with me?"

"Cool. When?" he asked.

"Now," I said. I knew it probably sounded crazy but I was already out.

Young laughed into the phone. "You serious? Like right now? Where at?" he asked.

"There's an old movie house that's now an independent movie theatre. It's over on 12th avenue by the water. The area is still under construction so there's not a lot of people over there. How about that?" I asked. I was surprised that the thought hadn't come to me before. I wasn't the biggest fan of foreign and independent movies but it would be the perfect place to go.

"Aight, see you there in half an hour," Young said.

"Ok," I said. We got off the phone and I couldn't help but wonder what I'd gotten myself into.

CHAPTER 8

I KNEW that it was bad but I didn't regret how things had worked out with Reggie. He didn't know it but I'd been as nice about it as I could be. Some of my friends just ghosted guys and stopped responding to their messages. I knew that I probably should have mentioned something to him before the date but I needed that second one to make sure that my feelings were right. It had worked out in my favor though. I was glad that I'd committed to not letting my night or outfit go to waste. I was ready to go meet Young.

I ended up taking a cab over to the movie theater. I wasn't in too much of a rush but it was too long for me to walk. The entire time I was heading over I couldn't help but think of what it was gonna be like to finally hang out with Young in a real setting. I wasn't nervous or anything like that. I think it was a mixture of curiosity and anxiety.

When I got to the theater I headed straight inside. I decided that it would probably be best for me to just go into a theater and wait for him there. I didn't want it to look like I was waiting for anyone, especially not Young. I looked at the descriptions for the movies and finally ended up picking some French movie with subtitles. It was described as some kind of romance so I was down with it.

It wasn't too late or too early. The theater wasn't too packed, thankfully. They only showed foreign and independent movies so it never got as crowded as the normal theatres did. I found a seat close to the back and close to a wall. There were only a handful of other people sprinkled through the theater, mostly couples. I was one of only two people there alone. I gave Young a quick call and let him know where I was sitting and in which theater.

The movie came on and I found myself strangely drawn to it. I'd expected some kind of boring film but instead it was pretty good. The movie was about a young woman from Paris trying to find her way through life and love. She was a young 20 something who had just completed her master's degree. She was being charmed by one of her former professors and was trying not to fall for him. I could relate to the struggle and adventure of it all. It felt like the movie could have been about me. I felt a connection to the woman on the screen. Our languages were different but we were going through the same things. I wasn't chasing a professor or anything but I was trying not to fall for Young and was failing miserably.

Much to my surprise I'd gotten pretty into the movie.. I didn't know how much time had passed but I almost forgot that I was waiting for Young. The girl on the screen was going through it, confiding in her friends that she'd slept with him. That was until I felt a presence and then the door to the theater opened.

He looked like something out of a movie at first. From where I was sitting I had a perfect view of the door and Young looked like some kind of movie hero...or villain as his tall frame stood in the darkness. I raised my hand and waved at him so he knew where I was. He walked all the way inside and made his way over to me. He moved slowly, yet deliberately. It was like he was trying to get to me and keep me waiting at the same time. I tried to keep my nerves calm through.

Young finally got all the way to me and sat down next to me. His scent arrived just as he did and the smell of his sweet perfume wafted up my nose and made me feel intoxicated. It was a familiar scent but I didn't know from where. I just knew that I really liked it. Young looked as good as he smelled, dressed in a pair of jeans and a thin sweater that showed off his well-defined arms. It was dark but he seemed to have a glow around him.

Young sat down beside me and leaned over to me. "Hey pretty lady, fancy meeting you here," Young said. It was clearly the last thing that I was expecting. I turned my head towards him, confusion written all over my face. He smiled at me, showing off a set of perfect teeth. I giggled. To have Young's reputation for being this feared gang leader and stuff, he sure didn't seem like it. He was full of surprises: first our phone conversation and then his little greeting.

Young licked his full lips and leaned a little closer to me. When he opened his mouth to speak, his warm breath wrapped itself around my neck and it sent a quick shiver through my body. If just the feeling of his breath that close to my neck was doing that much to me, imagine what would happen if he actually got the chance to put those lips on me. "My bad for being late. I got caught up with something," he said.

"It's cool. I actually like the movie," I whispered back.

It got a little awkward then and we both opted to just watch the movie. The woman on the screen was a 20-something-year-old, just like me. She was on a date with some guy and it was going well, almost too well. She was wondering when something was going to go wrong.

I turned my head to Young to say something about the scene but he'd also turned his head at the same time. Because of how close we were to one another, our lips brushed. It was a quick thing but the electricity that passed between us was enough to charge us up. Young pressed himself closer to me and our little brush became a full on passionate kiss. Our lips were pushing back and forth against one another and I was loving every minute of it. I felt like I was back in high school or something.

We kept on kissing for a little while longer until we naturally broke it up. It was the same thing that happened at the club that night. We just knew when it was time.

Young reached down and grabbed my hand and held it for the rest of the movie. I didn't know if he enjoyed it or not but I liked it. I was really just enjoying the moment. Young and I kept whispering to one another about the movie and it was cool to see that he wasn't one dimensional. I didn't know a lot of dudes who were willing to sit through an almost two hour movie where they had to read everything.

The movie finally ended and the few other people in the theater started to get up to leave. Neither Young or I made any moves to get up. We were still sitting there hand in hand when the last person left.

"What's up next?" Young asked. The look on his face wasn't expecting but I knew that he was down with whatever. Truthfully, I was finding that I was having a hard time not doing anything with him right then and there. The kiss that he'd planted on me had been nothing but a teaser and I thought it was about time that I got the full attraction.

I smirked at him. "It's not past your bedtime?" I asked. "You don't have business hours?"

"All my hours are business hours," Young said with confidence. I stood up and so did he.

"There's a hotel close to here," I said. For the second time that night I was letting myself just be free. I'd called Young on a whim and I was about to do something else with him on a whim too. "I can't remember the exact name but it's on the corner about 10 blocks down this avenue." I looked down at my phone to check the time. "I want you to meet me there in 45 minutes. I'll call you in 20 with a room number."

If Young was surprised or even taken aback by anything that I was saying, he kept it to himself. He eyed me curiously and nodded when I was finished. I turned to leave, heading to go grab another taxi and wondering about what I was about to do.

CHAPTER 9

AFTER I LEFT the movie theater I headed straight for the hotel that I'd mentioned to Young. I didn't know what he'd be doing while he waited for my call but I was feeling nervous. It wasn't enough to stop me from doing anything though. I got out of my cab and headed into the hotel.

It was just as nice on the inside as it looked from the outside. The lobby was huge with super high ceilings and was decorated in a modern style. I liked the decor.

I approached the front desk and spoke to the guy behind the counter. He was really friendly and helped me get everything done quickly. It didn't seem like he was judging me either and I know that probably had to be hard to do. A woman coming into the hotel in the middle of the night asking for a room had to look a certain kind of way to people but he kept any comments he had to himself. Once I got everything with the room situated I headed upstairs to it. I gave Young a quick call, letting him know that I was on the 8th floor in room 830.

The hotel room itself was pretty standard. It was set up like any normal room would be, big bed, nightstands, etc. The standout was the beautiful view of the Hudson River and New Jersey.

The conversation that they'd been having in the beauty salon popped into my mind as I paced the room nervously. I could hear both sides of the debate in my head and they were making me rethink my decision. Was I doing something wrong by sleeping with Young so soon? I don't know what it was about him that made me so eager to do it but I'd pretty much made up my mind about it. We hadn't even had a real "getting to know you" conversation or anything yet but it didn't matter. The more I sat there thinking about it, the more I just decided to say fuck it and get it started. At the end of the day the only thing I could trust were my feelings and this felt right.

I felt like somebody out of a sitcom or something like that. I was trying to figure out how I was gonna open the door up for Young. How sexy did I want to be? Should my clothes be on or off? Should I let him come to me or should I go to him? I kept on asking myself questions and damn near gave myself a headache. I realized that I just needed to stop talking and just go with the flow because it wouldn't be that long before he got to the room.

I decided that I'd just keep it simple. I stripped down to my bra and panties, thankful that I put on a matching set. The hotel had a little store in the lobby and I'd stopped on my way upstairs to get some stuff for the night—a toothbrush, lotion, condoms, stuff like that. In the bathroom I found two white bathrobes. I put one of them on, slipping it over my skin. I looked in the mirror and let the robe fall off of my shoulders a little bit and posed in a sexy way. It was coming together but I was missing something. I didn't have a scarf or anything to wrap my hair so I just tired it up on top of my head in a loose bun. I checked myself in the mirror again and I had to admit that I liked the way it all came together. It wasn't the best that I could do but given what I had, it was great. I reapplied my lip gloss and made sure that my makeup didn't look crazy.

I finished everything up right on time too. There was a knock on the door and it couldn't have been anyone but Young. I called out to him letting him know that I'd be right there. I was nervous but I was just going to go with it. I looked in the mirror one last time to make sure that I was good and then headed to the door.

I slowly opened the door to the room after double checking that it was him. I'd lowered the top of the robe a little bit, nothing too crazy but just enough to give him a peak. It worked too. His eyes had gone straight for my body after I opened the door. He walked in and I pushed the door closed behind him.

The sound of the door closing might as well have been the signal for us to start. Young took a step closer to me and put one hand behind my back. He stepped closer to me and leaned down, planting a soft, passionate kiss right on my lips. I kissed him back, letting my guard fall as I did. He broke the kiss after a few moments.

"Damn," he said breathlessly, "I wanted to do that since I first saw you at the police station."

I didn't have any words for him. I was still in his arms looking up at him. Instead of speaking, I tip toed up to him and kept right on kissing him. As soft as his lips looked, it was nothing in comparison to how soft they actually were.

While I kept on kissing him, I used my free hands to grab at his belt and buckle. Young slipped the sweater that he had on over his head. He was wearing a wifebeater underneath. After a couple of moments of struggling, I managed to undo it all. Young's pants dropped to his knees. He broke out kiss to step out of them and took of his undershirt too. He was wearing a pair of black boxer briefs and socks, nothing else. His long, thick, muscular legs looked huge in the underwear. Thick thighs led up to a growing bulge.

I was still wearing my robe but it was time

for that to change. I did a slow and sexy walk over to the bed. I left Young standing in front of the door as I made my way over. I never turned around to face him but when I got to the foot of the bed I slowly undid the belt of the robe. I pulled it off shoulder by shoulder and then finally let it fall to the ground. I climbed up onto the bed, making sure he had a nice view of my ass. I posed on all fours for a little bit before I turned over onto my back.

It wasn't the best strip tease in the world but as I looked at Young, I could tell that it had been more than enough. The bulge in his underwear had grown. He rubbed at it and then put his hand inside. He pulled out his dick and started to stroke it as he looked at me. It was long, thick, black, and looked like it could do some damage.

Young threw the boxer briefs off that he was wearing and walked over to me, dick first. He pulled me to the edge of the bed and slowly slipped my panties off. Young had big, strong hands but he moved with a certain delicateness that I appreciated. Once my panties were all the way off, he climbed into bed with me. We started kissing and he positioned himself between my legs.

It had been a while since I had some and Young's dick was bigger than normal. He had to be really careful when he was pushing it in but once it was all the way inside it felt amazing. Young held his weight above me and I caressed each of his muscles on his well-defined body. He worked himself in and out of me as we kissed. I moaned loudly. I wasn't trying to at first but it felt so damn good that it couldn't be helped. He was beating it up right.

Young grabbed at my legs and pushed them further up. He held my ankles as I watched his pelvis grind into me. I held up my hands to try and get him to slow down a little bit but I think he knew that I was really enjoying it. Young was hitting every spot that I needed hit and then some.

We'd switched positions a couple of times but it didn't really matter. Young didn't skip a beat. No matter which way we moved he just kept right on going and I loved every minute of it. When I finally thought that I wouldn't be able to take it much longer, he announced that he was close to coming. I was as well. Young and I both reached our climaxes at the same time. My body shook and his went rigid as all of the emotions that had been building up inside of us for a while finally exploded.

We got cleaned up and then climbed into bed. He was laying on his back and much to my surprise he pulled me closer to him so that we could cuddle. I put my head on his chest and he wrapped a muscular arm around me.

"Are you from Harlem?" I asked him. There was enough silence between us and at that moment it didn't seem like either of us was about to go to sleep.

"Yeah, born and raised," Young said. "I love Harlem. I've seen and been through a lot out here."

"Same here," I said.

"Nah, you must not be in Harlem like that then. Cause I'd have remembered seeing you before," Young said.

"I go everywhere," I said.

"Oh, excuse me," Young said with a little laugh. My head was still on his chest and my hand was on his ripped stomach so every move he made, I felt. I didn't mind it at all as I ran my fingers over his abs. "You real fancy out here."

"Not at all," I said. "I love the whole city so

I just go wherever. My friends pick places and I just go."

"I feel you," he said. "I wish I had that kind of freedom."

"Why don't you?" I asked.

"Responsibilities," he said. "You know nothing crazy like kids and shit but business is always business. I can't forget that."

I wanted to ask about his business and stuff but I didn't know how it would go over. Just because neither of us addressed the elephant in the room didn't mean it didn't exist. I wasn't about to mess up the moment by bringing it up though.

"I get that," I said. "You wanna hear something funny?"

"What?" He asked.

"I kept thinking I was seeing you out," I admitted. "I was getting my hair done and I thought I saw you." I told him about how I thought I kept running into him.

"Nah, it was me," he said.

"Really?" I asked.

"Yeah, I'm pretty sure it was me," Young said. "You not bugging out like that."

"That's good to know," I said. "I thought it was me being in my head."

"Hmm, maybe it was me in your head since you kept seeing me," Young said. I couldn't see his face in the dark but I knew he had to be smirking.

We kept talking for a few more minutes...until I drifted off mid conversation. It wasn't intentional at all but I didn't realize how tired I was. Young had really put it on me and that had put me to sleep. I felt him kiss me on the forehead in my dreams.

When I got up the next morning, it took me a couple of minutes to figure out where I was. After I got my bearings and figured out that I was with Young and it was Sunday morning, I figured that I needed to go. It felt good to wake up in his arms but I needed to get my ass back to my own house and out of the hotel.

I was being as quiet as I could be, almost silent, as I got dressed. I found my panties and was happy to see that my dress wasn't wrinkled at all, despite laying across the back of a chair all night long. I slipped it on and was just about to put my shoes on when Young's voice scared me.

"Where are you going Tae?" His voice was extra deep as he rolled over. I was sitting on the edge of the bed and he reached out and put an arm around my midsection.

"I gotta go, but I can't wait till we see each other again," I said. I meant it too. I finished putting my shoes on and before I left, Young and I shared another passionate kiss.

CHAPTER 10

IT HAD BEEN two weeks since everything happened with Young and I at the hotel and I had to admit that things seemed to be going good. I wasn't trying to get ahead of myself but Young just made himself so easy to talk to. We chilled out two more times in those two weeks but it was more of the quality vs the quantity of times.

I'd spent the last two weekends with Young. I mean the entire weekend. I left work on Friday and he'd come straight to my house and wouldn't leave until it was time for me to leave for my shift on Monday. I was being as secure as possible while I was sneaking around with Young, but he understood it, though.

Both of the weekends that Young and I spent together were amazing. We didn't leave for anything, not even food. I didn't ask about his business and he didn't tell me. I probably should have wondered how someone like him could just take time away and stay in the house but he kept his phone near him in case of an emergencies. I knew it had to sound stupid to some people but I'd almost been thinking about turning my badge in and going over to the dark side just for Young.

Each time we spent a weekend together, it wasn't just any specific part of it that made it good. We didn't even leave the apartment to go get food; we just ordered in. Young and I had some of the best sex that I'd ever had in my life. That man knew exactly how to use his body and I knew it too. That first night at the hotel hadn't really been anything. Young had worked me out in a bunch of different positions in a lot of ways.

We were building a real connection with one another. We talked for hours, about anything. We spoke about life, the world, the two of us. We watched movies and listened to music. I didn't want to ruin either of our weekends together so I didn't ask but in the back of my mind I kept wondering about Young's note. He had at least one person working for him on the inside of the police department and I wanted to know who it was. I wondered if the person was an ally or could even be a friend.

"Damn, that shit was good," Young said as he laid his head back on the pillow. I was looking down at him from my position as my legs straddled his body. I'd just finished riding the hell out of him and as always, he kept right up with me.

I climbed off of him, not even caring that my titties were just dangling in his face. I laid down next to him resting my head on his arm. Young started stroking my hair, something that he loved to do.

"I like this," Young said. It sounded as though he'd just made a decision or something.

"Like what?" I asked.

"*This*," he said as he waved his other hand around and then landed it on me. "What we doing. This stuff. I like you. I could get used to this," Young said. He kissed me on the forehead and I smiled.

"Me too," I said. "Thank you for letting me come to your spot for a change."

We'd spent the last two weekends at my apartment. It was almost the natural thing to do; me bringing him to my crib. It didn't even cross my mind to go to his. I didn't know what it was going to be like or what to expect.

"It's cool," Young said. "I can trust you here."

"That means a lot," I said. It did. Our circumstances were strange but I thought we were making the best of them. "Do you bring people here a lot?"

"Nah," Young shook his head, "not at all."

"Why not?" I asked him.

"Information is a funny thing. You always gotta be careful about who knows what," he said. Young had this way of speaking at times that made it clear to me why he was a leader. It had nothing to do with violence, murder, or intimidation. People followed him because he gave off the image of someone to follow. He just always seemed like he had it together, even if he didn't. "Now, you a little different because you could've looked all this up in a computer some-where probably. But with other people who can't access that information, how do they find out where I live?

"You'd have to tell them," I said.

"Or someone else would have to," he said. "It's not about being secretive, it's about being safe. Nobody can tell you something they don't know. Not to mention that sometimes a nigga just wanna be alone. I get tired of all that Young shit sometimes. I can come here and just be Eric and listen to my music and shit."

I nodded my head. I didn't fully understand what he was saying because it wasn't a life that I'd had to live but anyone could relate to wanting to come home to their peace. I just didn't have a secret identity like he did. "That makes sense," I said. "So, since Young isn't here right now, can Eric get me some Chipotle?"

Young busted out laughing. "You really want Chipotle? My little speech made you hungry?"

"Not even. Something else did," I said playfully.

Young grabbed me and started planting peck kisses on my neck. "I got something I could feed you," he said in a seductive way.

"'I'll have that for dessert," I said. "They're still open for like an hour and a half. Would you mind boo?"

Young sat up and took the cover off of him.

He was still naked and his body looked powerful as he walked across the room to grab his under-wear. "Of course not. That's an easy ask. I'll hop in a cab there and be right back."

"Thanks," I said. "I'll wait here."

"Where else you gonna go?" Young asked. He pecked me on the lips before he left.

While I sat around waiting for him to come back, I decided to get up and freshen up. I'd brought my overnight bag with me so I had all of my usual toiletries. I took a quick shower and when I got out I put on a pair of sweatpants after lotioning my body and tying up my hair. I was actually really hungry so I was hoping that he would have been back by the time I got out but he wasn't.

I decided to go and look around, hoping to learn a little more about Young. It wasn't snoop-ing, at least not to me. I wasn't going to go through any of his stuff. I just wanted to brush the surface of who he was. I looked at the pictures he had on the wall. I didn't know who the people in the photos were but there were some of Young at various stages of growing up and with different people.

I kept looking at the pictures all over the

house but gasped when I recognized a familiar face in one of them with Young. Officer Willie Harris and Young were standing together in a picture with one another. Harris worked in my department. I'd seen him around a couple of times and had a couple of small conversation with him. The picture of him and Young showed the two of them standing next together as Harris held a plaque that shower Class of 2010. I didn't know how the two of them knew one another but I was sure at that point that my ally in the precinct was none other than Officer Harris. I wasn't planning on asking him about it though. I didn't know if Harris was working for Young or if his giving me the note was a one-time thing. I decided that the less I knew about the situation the better.

When Young finally came back in a couple of minutes later, I was sitting on the couch waiting for him. I decided to be a little playful when he came back in.

"Where have you been?" I asked with a fake attitude. I'd crossed my legs and folded my arms like I was mad.

"What you talkin 'bout?" Young asked in confusion.

"You heard me," I said. "I been sitting in here all this time waiting for this food. I could have passed out. I could have died." I sucked my cheeks in like I'd lost weight in the few minutes since he'd been gone. He caught on and started to laugh at me. I joined in. I liked that we could be goofy around each other.

Young closed and locked the door behind him. He set the food down on the dining table and I walked over to him. He'd gotten himself a burrito bowl too and took them both out of the bag before balling it up.

"I must have stood up too fast," I said as I stopped walking. I placed my hand on my stomach.

"What's going on?" Young asked.

"Nothing serious. Just a little nausea from nowhere," I said. The nausea got worse, so much worse that I had to run to the bathroom. I felt like I was going to throw up. I got to the bathroom and closed the door behind me as I dropped to my knees. I threw my hair over my shoulder just in time. Everything that I'd eaten and drank that day came out and into the toilet. It was disgusting to see and felt even worse.

When I was finished I flushed the toilet and

stood up to brush my teeth. I was trying to figure out if I'd eaten anything that might have messed up my stomach but I couldn't think of anything. I'd eaten sushi for lunch but it was a place that I'd been a hundred times before. When it finally hit me I almost dropped my toothbrush.

I finished up in the bathroom and slowly made my way out to where Young was. He was sitting at the table and had laid out both of our food but hadn't started eating.

"You good?" He asked me.

I didn't say anything so he asked again, a little louder this times. "Tae, is everything good? You need anything from me?"

I took a seat across from him, not really believing what I was about to say. "I didn't think anything was wrong when my period was late. It just does that sometimes. But now that I'm throwing up…" My voice trailed off. Young's eyes had gone wide and then back to their normal size.

I could tell that he knew what I was saying but he still just had to ask. "What are you saying?" He asked.

I took a deep breath and looked him in the

eyes. "I'm saying that I know you just came back inside but I need to go to the store again and get me a pregnancy test."

The look on Young's face was one of concern. If he had other thoughts then he kept them to himself. "I got you," he said. He stood up and walked out the door, leaving me alone at the table with confusion.

Find out what happens next in part two of Cuffed To A Savage! Available Now!

To find out when Mia Black has new books available, **follow Mia Black on Instagram: @authormiablack**

CUFFED TO A SAVAGE 2

Tae knew she shouldn't have let it happen, but it did. Now, she has to somehow find a way to keep her relationship a secret, especially when Young is under investigation. As officers try to find enough evidence to send him away for a long time, Tae fears that her secret will be revealed. Not only will she lose her job, she'll lose the man she can't help but love.

Will her bad decision lead to disaster?

Find out what happens next in part two of Cuffed To A Savage!

To find out when Mia Black has new books available, **follow Mia Black on Instagram: @authormiablack**

Made in the USA
Monee, IL
24 May 2021